My Ancestors'
Wildest
Dreams

Written by Ava Holloway and Amanda Lynch

Illustrated by Bonnie Lemaire

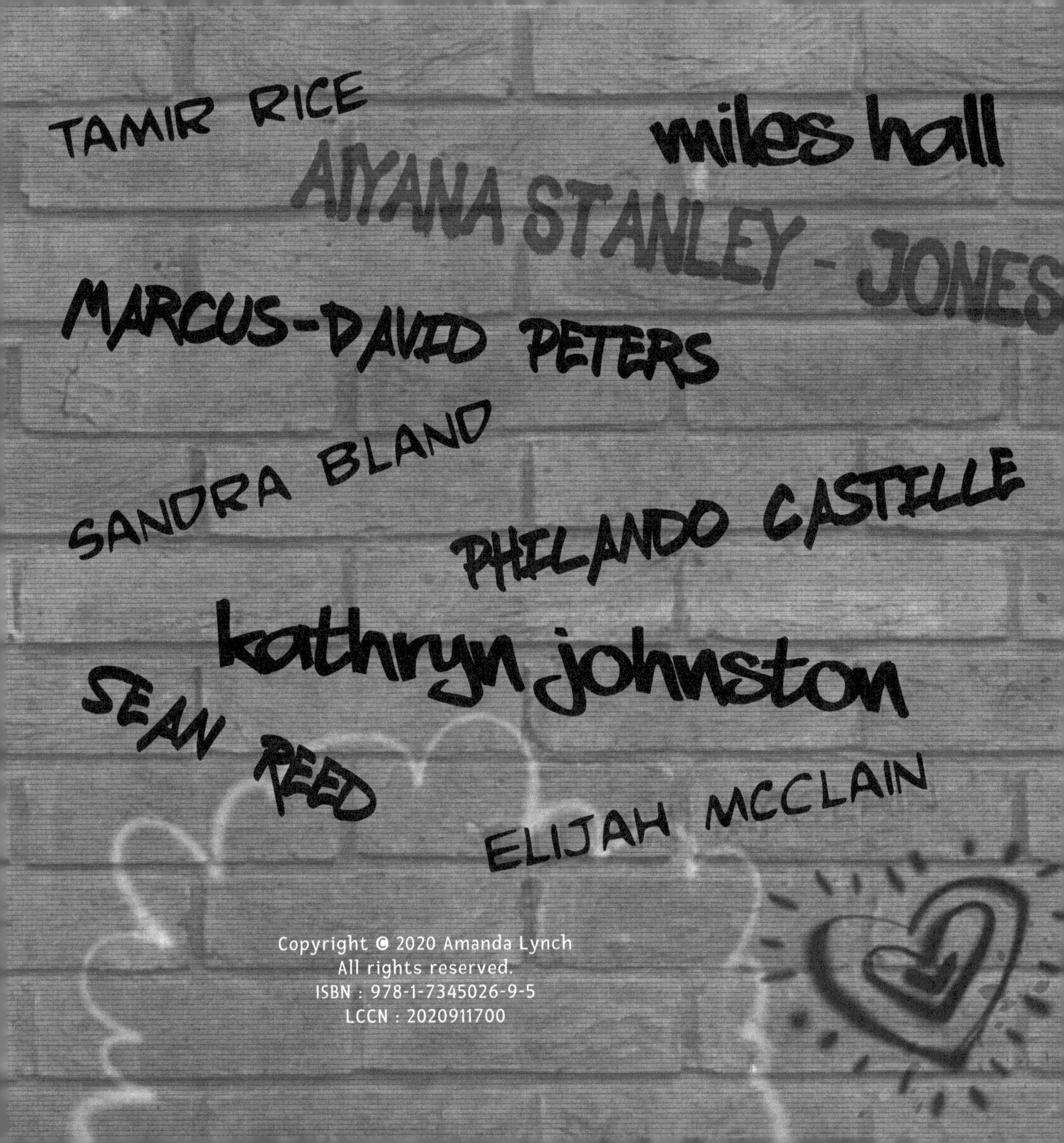

TAMIR RICE
miles hall
AIYANA STANLEY - JONES
MARCUS-DAVID PETERS
SANDRA BLAND
PHILANDO CASTILLE
kathryn johnston
SEAN REED
ELIJAH MCCLAIN

ISBN : 978-1-7345026-9-5
LCCN : 2020911700

This book is dedicated to all of the beautiful brown dancers in my life who have made this book possible. My brother, Amani Justin Holloway, thank you for letting me tag along with you to dance classes and for teaching me what it means to be a dancer both in and outside of the studio. Tahlia, Jaiden, Hazy, and Rosebud, thank you for being the best siblings a girl could ask for. My parents and step-parents, thank you for seeing my light. My grandparents, thank you for always being there. My cousin, Alesandra Harper, for showing me that this was possible. Ms. Wyatt, thank you for teaching me to express myself in ways I would not have thought of before. Ms. Anne and my CVDA family, thank you for being my second family and home. Ms. Sheena, Ms. Brandee, and Ms. Gin, thank you for always challenging me. My St. Catherine's family and friends, thank you for believing in me. -Love, Ava

This book is dedicated to my ancestors. You can never enslave the human spirit. Omambala bu anyi bia. Orimiri Omambala ka anyi ga ejina. -Love, Amanda

AHMAUD ARBERY   ALBERTA SPRUILL

ELEANOR BUMPERS

BREONNA TAYLOR

Brown ballerina on the world's stage,
Using your voice and your gifts to promote change,

Know that they see you and you can do anything.
Refuse to be moved until freedom rings.

Brown ballerina with your pineapple puff,

Made with strength, courage, and pride,

You are more than enough.

Relevé

Plié

Plié

Sauté

Keep dancing for change;
don't let anything get in your way.

Brown ballerina,

you are your ancestors' wildest dreams.

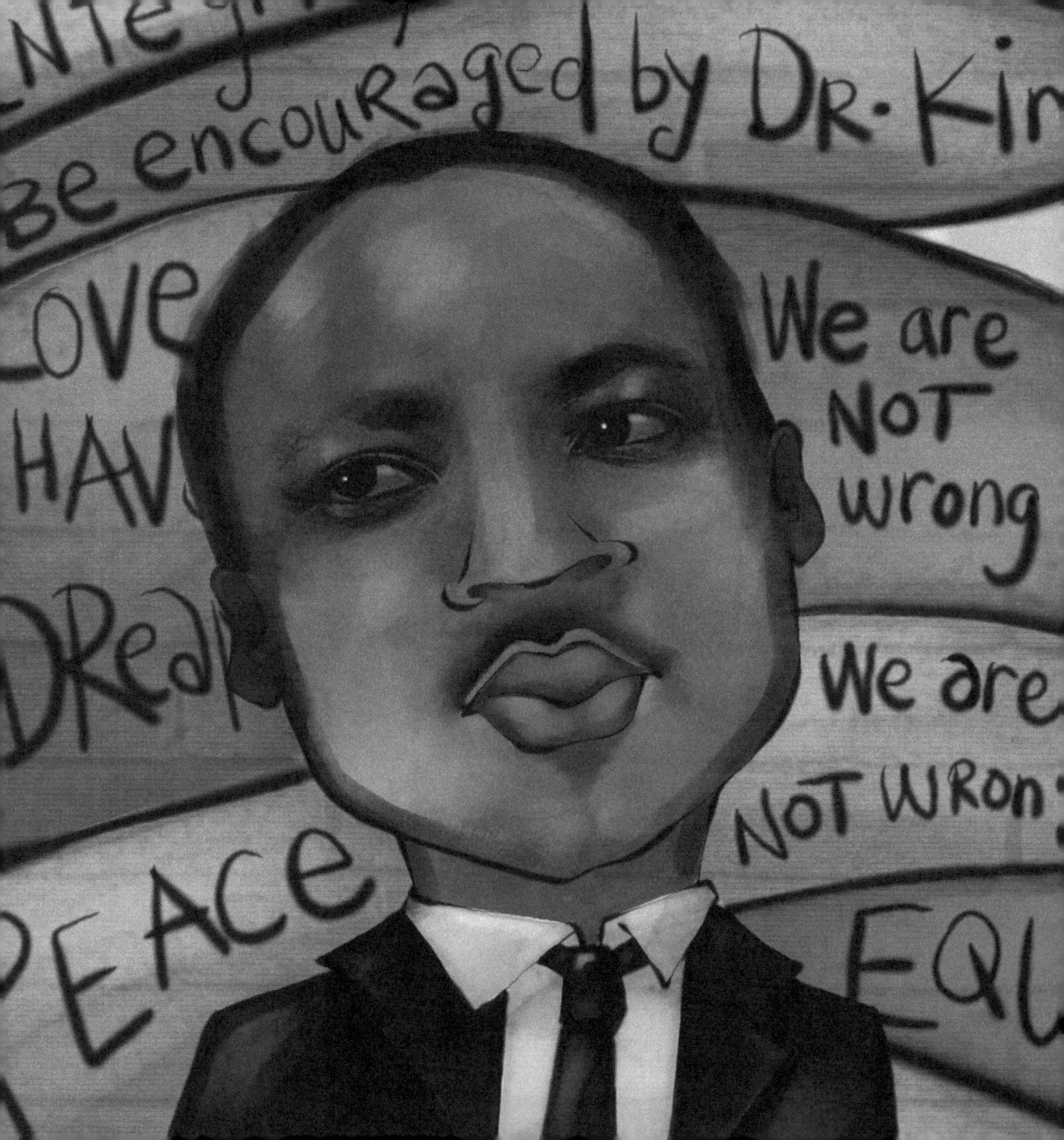
Be encouraged by DR.
We are NOT wrong
We are
NOT
PEACE

Grab every laurel and continue to be the change you want to see.

Be encouraged by the words of Dr. King, "We are not wrong! We are not wrong!"

Let mighty justice roll down and be your heartsong.

Cities burning, mothers heartsick,
Communities hurting, there is no quick fix.

The fight for justice en pointe takes time to achieve,

But with hard work and consistency

you can do anything.

Be the changemaker
you were created to be,

Brown ballerina, standing tall,
staring down General Robert E. Lee.

Replace false idols with real ones.
Let them watch and see.
Shout from the rooftops, "Lift every voice and sing!"

Take a deep breath, tendu, deep plié.

Change will come through what you do and say.

Brown ballerina with your pineapple puff,

Be the change you wish to see.

Refuse to be moved until freedom rings.

Brown ballerina,

dance on.

Remember Who You Are

1. You are brave.
2. You are strong.
3. You are more than enough.
4. You are proud.
5. You are kind.
6. You are hard-working.
7. You are honest.
8. You are thankful.
9. You are silly.
10. You are in control of your feelings.
11. You are smart.
12. You are helpful.
13. You are a good friend.
14. You are curious.
15. You are resilient.
16. You are talented.
17. You are a great problem solver.
18. You are a winner.
19. You are joyous.
20. You are peaceful.
21. You are safe.
22. You are healthy.
23. You are confident.
24. You are worthy.
25. You are a star.
26. You are deserving.
27. You are trustworthy.
28. You are amazing.
29. You are consistent.
30. You are capable.
31. You are a leader.
32. You are a dream-maker.
33. You are open-minded.
34. You are your own superhero.
35. You are free to make your own choices.
36. You are perfect just the way you are.
37. You are complete.
38. You are your ancestors' wildest dreams.
39. You are quick-witted.
40. You are assertive.
41. You are a thinker.
42. You are true to yourself.
43. You are deserving.
44. You are a giver.
45. You are loved.
46. You are mindful.
47. You are grateful.
48. You are a fighter.
49. You are an advocate for others.
50. You are generous.
51. You are thoughtful.
52. You are insightful.
53. You are extraordinary.
54. You are remarkable.
55. You are unique.
56. You are valued.
57. You are creative.
58. You are powerful.

59. You are happy.
60. You are gifted.
61. You are determined.
62. You are true to yourself.
63. You are able.
64. You are balanced.
65. You are compassionate.
66. You are magical.
67. You are worth it.
68. You are content.
69. You are comfortable.
70. You are free.
71. You are okay.
72. You are here.
73. You are wise.
74. You are adventurous.
75. You are in charge of how you feel today. Choose happiness.
76. You are calm.
77. You are an activist.
78. You choose your own path.
79. You are present.
80. You are successful.
81. You are reliable.
82. You are a good student.
83. You are responsible.
84. You are caring.
85. You are powerful.
86. You are passionate about your goals.
87. You are a changemaker.

88. You are a doer.
89. You are adventurous.
90. You are able to work through difficult times.
91. You are able to manage "big feelings."
92. You are understanding.
93. You are contemplative.
94. You are energetic.
95. You are a young queen.
96. You are deserving of good things.
97. You are able to ask for help.
98. You are special.
99. You are courageous.
100. You are a visionary.

Dance terms:

plié (bend), relevé (rise), sauté (jump), tendu (stretch)

Dear Reader,

This book was inspired by Ava Holloway and Kennedy George, two ballerinas. Their photos were taken by Marcus Ingram and Julia Rendleman in front of the monument of Confederate General Robert E. Lee, in Richmond, Virginia. Ultimately, those photographs went viral, and this moment propelled the duo into a summer of activism and dance. Posed in traditional ballet attire, the friends had no idea that a chance encounter at the Lee Monument would catapult them into the spotlight while serving as a beacon of hope for millions of young activists around the world.

Ava Holloway has performed with Central Virginia Dance Academy since 2009, is co-founder of the dance group *Brown Ballerinas for Change*, and is a member of Joni at St. Catherine's School, where she was dance team co-captain and awarded the Creative Crystal Dance Award (2019-2020). Ava has found purpose in justice-seeking through dance and aspires to be a doctor. She dreams of saving lives. Ava enjoys hanging out with friends and making crazy dances.

Amanda Lynch is the author of best-selling children's books, *The Mindfulness Room, Breathe, Baby, Breathe: An ABC Guide to Mindfulness,* and *The 5-Minute Mindfulness Journal for Kids.* She enjoys yoga, advocating for others, and spending time with her children, Ava, Violet-Hazel, Primrose, and Justin.

CPSIA information can be obtained
at www.ICGtesting.com
Printed in the USA
BVHW020515220321
603058BV00002B/52